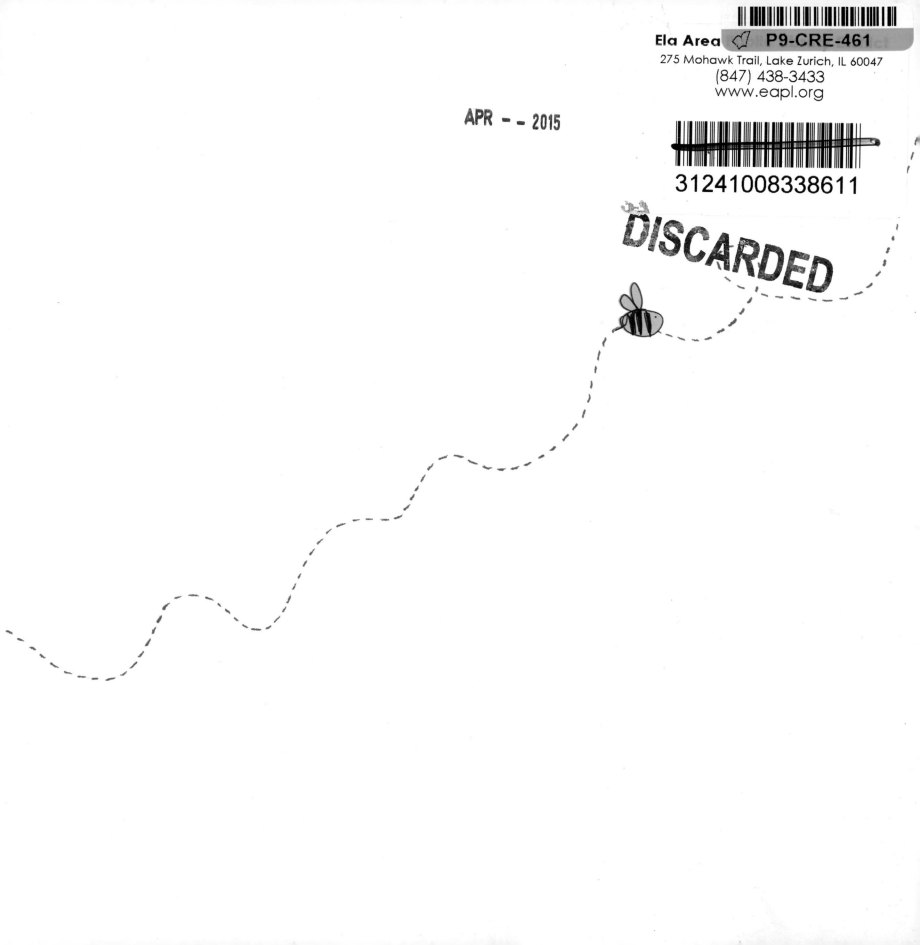

For Charles and his very special grandson

First published in 2014 by Child's Play (International) Ltd
Ashworth Road, Bridgemead, Swindon SN5 7YD UK

Published in USA by Child's Play Inc
250 Minot Avenue, Auburn, Maine 04210

Distributed in Australia by Child's Play Australia Pty Ltd
Unit 10/20 Narabang Way, Belrose, NSW 2085

Text and illustrations copyright © 2014 Trudi Esberger
The moral right of the author/illustrator has been asserted

ISBN 978-1-84643-662-8
CLP300614CPL07146628

Printed in Shenzhen, China

1 3 5 7 9 10 8 6 4 2

A catalogue record of this book
is available from the British Library

www.childs-play.com

THE BOY WHO LOST HIS BUMBLE

TRUDI ESBERGER

Once there was a boy who
loved his garden.

He loved
the flowers,
he loved
the trees,

but most of all,
he loved the **bees**.

Bumble bee diary

Amir
likes pink flowers

Bob
very fuzzy

Holly
plays with Sue

Lin
very buzzy

Seb
loves dancing

Sue
likes playing hide and seek

The bees were always happy
and watching them made the boy happy too.

Then one day it started to rain
and the clouds began to **rumble**...
It was so wet, even the bees lost their **bumble.**

Without the bees, the boy
felt empty.

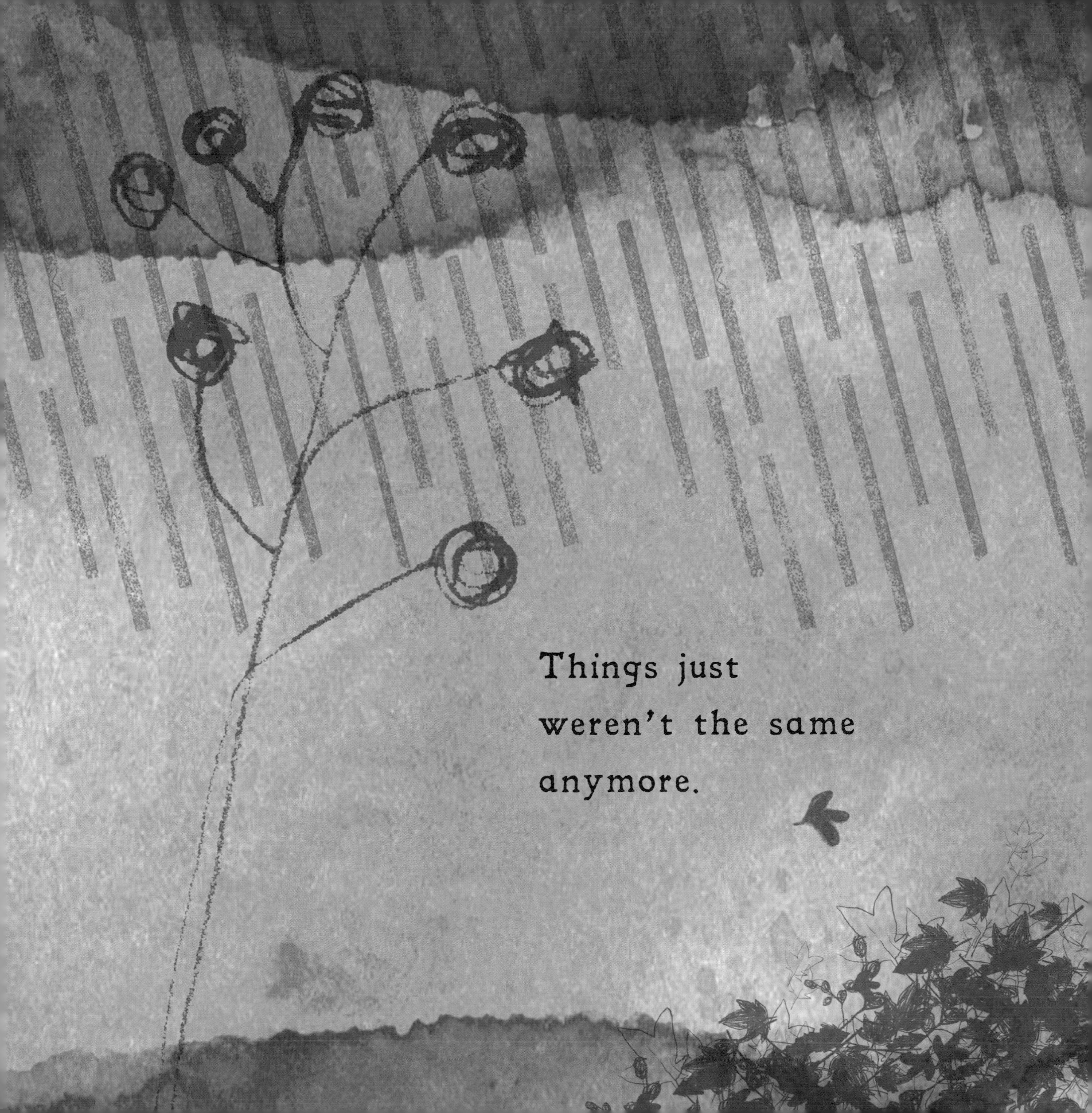

Things just
weren't the same
anymore.

He tried everything he could think of
to make them come back...

...but nothing worked.

One day, the garden **froze**
and the boy felt even emptier.

He wondered if the bees
would ever return.

He tried to keep busy with other things,
but it was no good.

He had almost given up hope when...

The sun rose ...

...and slowly...

...things started...

...to change.

The boy started to feel
a little less empty,

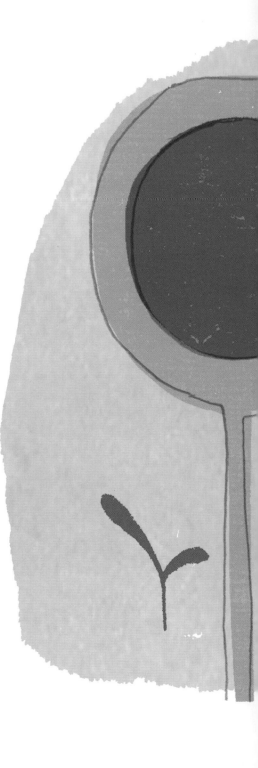

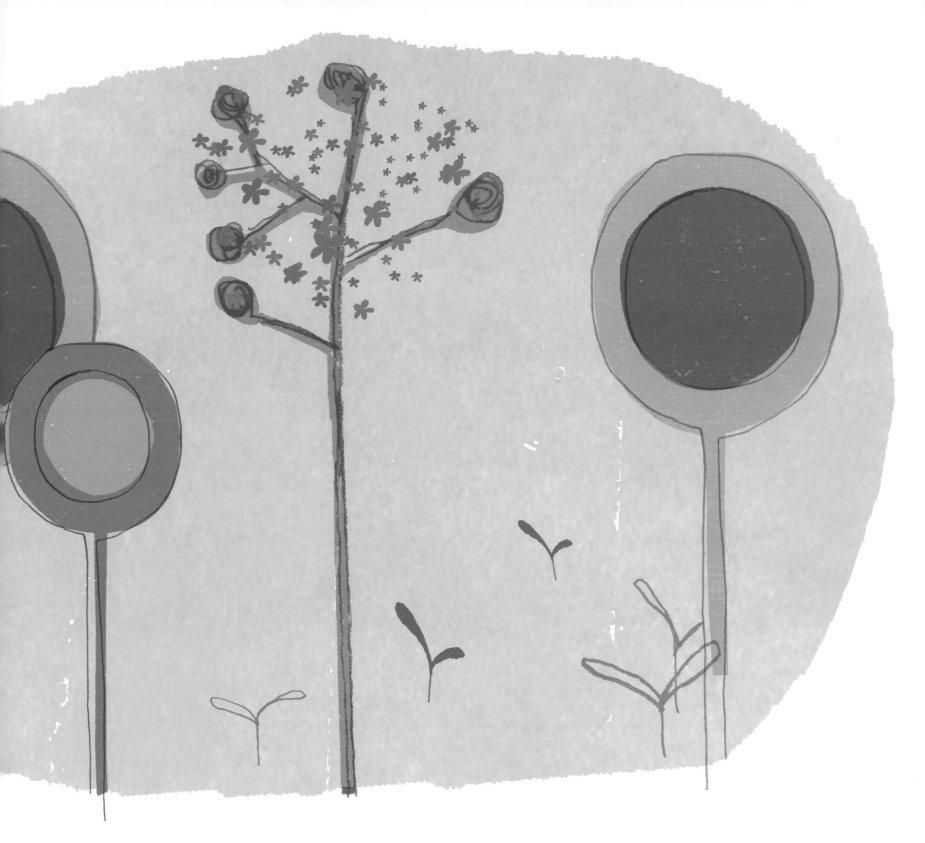

and before long...

bzzzzzzz

...he got his
bumble back.

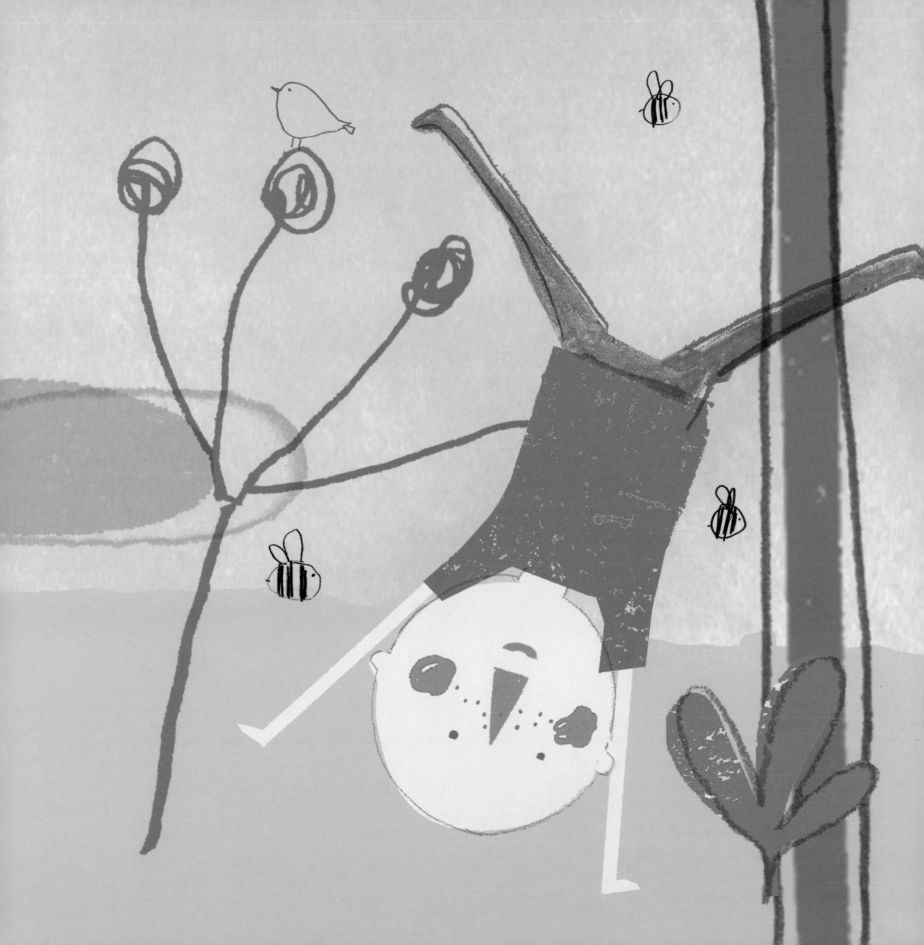

Perhaps bumbles  always come back.

Where do bumblebees go in winter?

At the end of the summer, a bumblebee colony dies out. Only the queen is left, and she hibernates somewhere safe and dry all through the winter.

under the garden shed

or in long grass

or even in a hole in the ground

The queen wakes up in spring, and feeds on flower nectar. She looks for a nest site in which to lay her eggs. These hatch into larvae, which spin cocoons after about two weeks. After two more weeks, they emerge as adult bees.

Why are bees important?

Pollen

Nectar

Bees pollinate trees, flowers, fruit and vegetables. Whilst collecting nectar and pollen, they move pollen from one plant to another. This fertilizes the plant's egg cell, which produces seeds, which grow into new plants. Bees pollinate about one third of the world's crops!

Bees are in trouble

Bees need flowers for food. But there are fewer wild flowers, fewer hedges and fewer wild spaces than there used to be. Bees have to travel further to find food. Fewer flowers mean fewer bees!

But YOU can help!

If you have a garden, plant lots of bee-friendly flowers. Choose plants that flower in different seasons, so that the bees have food all through the year. Don't use any bug sprays because these can harm bees.

Cornflower

Heather

Lavender

Foxglove

Leave a wild space in your garden where a queen bee might hibernate or find a good nest site. If you don't have a garden, look for spaces where you could sow some seeds.

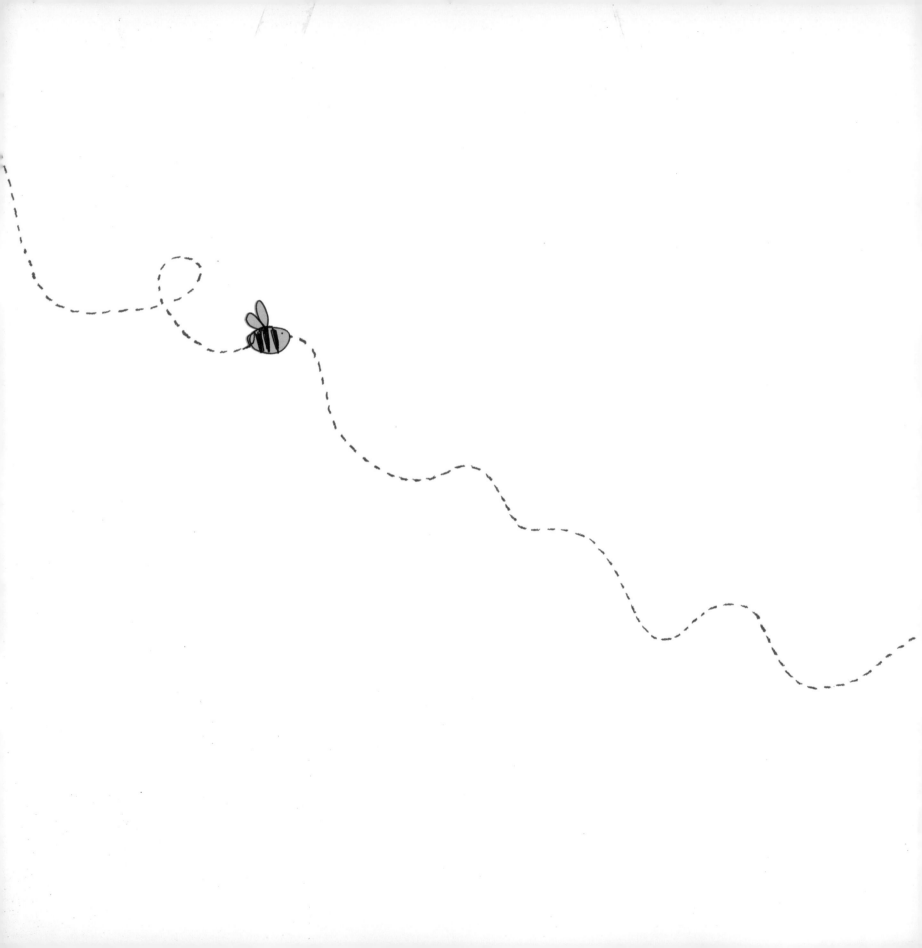